WALT DISNEY'S ALICE in Wonderland

Pictures by the Walt Disney Studio
Adapted by Al Dempster from the motion picture
based on the story by Lewis Carroll

 A GOLDEN BOOK · NEW YORK

Copyright © 1951, 2010 Disney Enterprises, Inc. All rights reserved. Published in the United States by
Golden Books, an imprint of Random House Children's Books, a division of Random House, Inc., 1745 Broadway,
New York, NY 10019, and in Canada by Random House of Canada Limited, Toronto, in conjunction with
Disney Enterprises, Inc. Originally published in slightly different form by Western Publishing Company,
Inc., in 1951. Golden Books, A Golden Book, A Little Golden Book, the G colophon,
and the distinctive gold spine are registered trademarks of Random House, Inc.
www.randomhouse.com/kids
Library of Congress Control Number: 2009925406
ISBN: 978-0-7364-2670-1
Printed in the United States of America
20 19

Alice was growing very tired, listening to her sister read. Just as her eyes began to close, she saw a white rabbit hurry by, looking at his pocket watch and talking to himself.

Alice thought that was very curious indeed—
a talking rabbit with a pocket watch! So she followed
him into a rabbit hole beneath a big tree.

And down she fell, down to the center of the
world, it seemed.

When Alice landed with a thump, the White
Rabbit was just disappearing through a door which
was much too small for her.

Alice drank from a bottle on the table and shrank away to a very tiny size. But now she could not reach the key to the little door!

At last Alice found a way to get through the little door. Seated on a bottle, she floated into Wonderland on a mysterious sea.

On through Wonderland Alice went,
looking for the White Rabbit. She met two jolly
fellows, Tweedle Dum and Tweedle Dee. They did
not know the Rabbit, so Alice hurried on.

At a neat little house in the woods,
at last she met the White Rabbit himself!

The Rabbit sent Alice into his little
house to hunt for his gloves. But instead she found
some cookies labeled Take One. So she did.

The cookie made Alice grow as big as the house. What a sight! Rabbit and his friend Dodo thought she was a dreadful monster.

Alice picked a carrot from Rabbit's garden. Eating it made her small again, so small that she was soon lost in a forest of grass.

Alice found herself in a garden of talking live flowers. There were bread-and-butterflies and rocking-horseflies, too.

Alice thought the garden was a pleasant place.
But the flowers thought Alice was just a weed, so
they would not let her stay.

Next Alice met a haughty Caterpillar blowing smoke rings. He told Alice to eat his mushroom if she wished to change her size.

Alice sampled one side, and shot up taller than the tree-tops, frightening the birds. But another bite made Alice just the right size.

"Now which way shall I go?" Alice wondered.
The signposts she found along the path were no
help—they pointed all over.

The signs on the tree read: YONDER, BACK, DOWN, THIS WAY, YONDER

"If I were looking for the White Rabbit, I'd ask the Mad Hatter," said a grinning Cheshire Cat up in a tree. "He lives down there."

Alice found the Mad Hatter and the March Hare celebrating their un-birthdays at a tea party. She joined them for a while.

After that nonsensical tea party, Alice wanted to go home. But none of the strange creatures seemed to know the way.

Alice wandered into the Queen's Garden. Soon, along came the Royal Procession. And who should be the royal trumpeter but the White Rabbit himself!

The Queen of Hearts asked Alice to play croquet. But Alice did not like the looks of the game.

"Off with her head!" cried the Queen.

Away Alice ran, while the army of cards gave chase, down all the tangled paths of Wonderland, and back to the riverbank.

"I'm glad to be back where things are really what they seem," said Alice as she woke up from her strange Wonderland dream.